FLIGHT TEST LAB
AIRPLANES

by Jackie Kramer
and Stuart Arden

Silver Dolphin
San Diego, California

For Lucy Grace

*Dedicated to **Sid Goldstein**, whose passion for airplanes inspired the dreams of thousands of schoolchildren.*

Silver Dolphin

Silver Dolphin Books
An imprint of the Advantage Publishers Group
5880 Oberlin Drive, San Diego, CA 92121-4794
www.silverdolphinbooks.com

Text copyright © 2003 by becker&mayer!

Flight Test Lab: Airplanes is produced by becker&mayer!,
Bellevue, Washington
www.beckermayer.com

If you have questions or comments about this product, send e-mail to
infobm@beckermayer.com

ISBN 1-59223-024-5

Produced, manufactured, and assembled in China.

3 4 5 6 7 09 08 07 06 05

04376

Edited by Ben Grossblatt
Art direction and design by Scott Westgard and Andrew Hess
Casewrap design by Scott Westgard
Illustrated by Joshua Beach (casewrap, pages 1–3, 24–27, 32),
Harry Whitver (pages 4–5), John Laidlaw (pages 8–9, 28–31),
Charles Floyd (pages 6–9), Michael Ingrassia (pages 10–11),
and Adam Crockett (pages 12–23)
Toy development by Todd Rider
Production management by Jennifer Marx
Facts checked by Paul Beck. Special thanks to Alissa Lenz.

Table of Contents

PREPARE FOR TAKEOFF

The Wright brothers made the first engine-powered flight about 100 years ago. But people have had their eyes on the skies for thousands of years, ever since man first admired a bird in flight. Many have dedicated their lives to the pursuit of flight or the promise of creating the perfect flying machine.

This book gets to the heart of the principles of flight, providing a pilot's-eye view of the skies—and of airplanes.

This Flight Test Lab comes with all the parts you'll need for assembling your own flying airplanes—even a battery-powered propeller winder! Build a jumbo jet, a sleek and sporty private aircraft, a fighter jet, and a sturdy prop plane. You can even mix and match the parts to create your own designs.

So turn the page and step into the hangar for a private tour of some massive, fast, slick, amphibious, stealthy, flexible, heroic, and gravity-defying machines.

Anatomy of an Airplane

Airplanes take many different forms, but they share similar parts and characteristics.

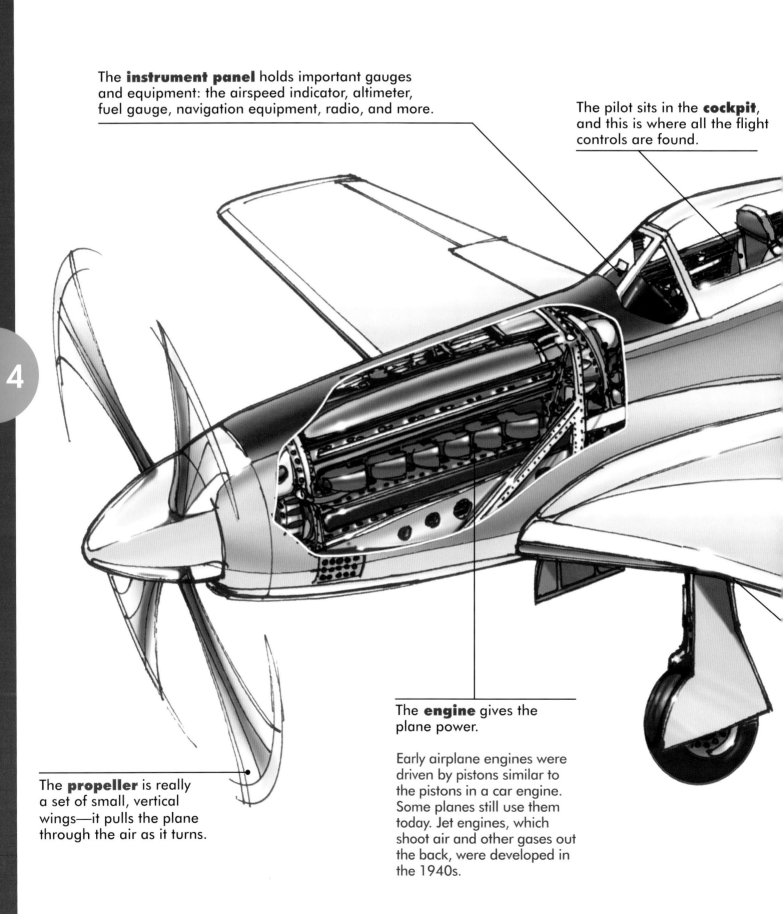

The **instrument panel** holds important gauges and equipment: the airspeed indicator, altimeter, fuel gauge, navigation equipment, radio, and more.

The pilot sits in the **cockpit**, and this is where all the flight controls are found.

The **engine** gives the plane power.

Early airplane engines were driven by pistons similar to the pistons in a car engine. Some planes still use them today. Jet engines, which shoot air and other gases out the back, were developed in the 1940s.

The **propeller** is really a set of small, vertical wings—it pulls the plane through the air as it turns.

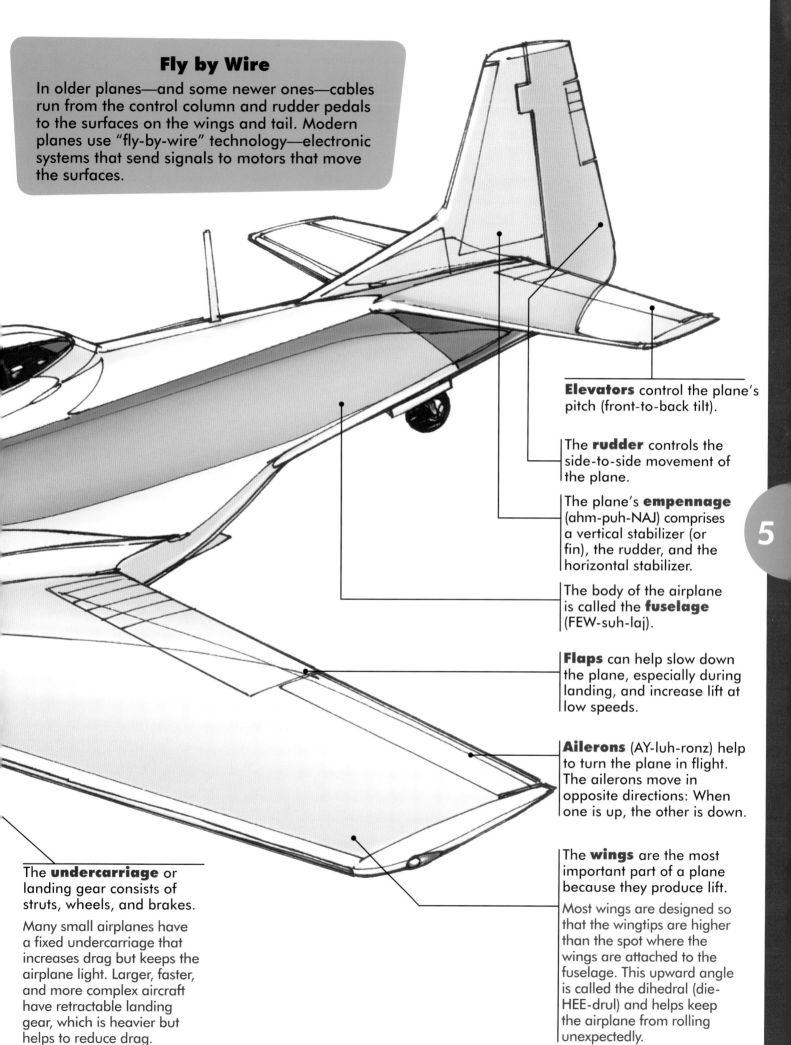

Elevators control the plane's pitch (front-to-back tilt).

The **rudder** controls the side-to-side movement of the plane.

The plane's **empennage** (ahm-puh-NAJ) comprises a vertical stabilizer (or fin), the rudder, and the horizontal stabilizer.

The body of the airplane is called the **fuselage** (FEW-suh-laj).

Flaps can help slow down the plane, especially during landing, and increase lift at low speeds.

Ailerons (AY-luh-ronz) help to turn the plane in flight. The ailerons move in opposite directions: When one is up, the other is down.

The **wings** are the most important part of a plane because they produce lift.

Most wings are designed so that the wingtips are higher than the spot where the wings are attached to the fuselage. This upward angle is called the dihedral (die-HEE-drul) and helps keep the airplane from rolling unexpectedly.

The **undercarriage** or landing gear consists of struts, wheels, and brakes.

Many small airplanes have a fixed undercarriage that increases drag but keeps the airplane light. Larger, faster, and more complex aircraft have retractable landing gear, which is heavier but helps to reduce drag.

Foundations of Flight

To understand flight, you need to understand the basics—
the four forces of flight and the three axes of rotation.

GRAVITY, LIFT, DRAG, AND THRUST

These are the four forces of flight. Lift and thrust work to propel the plane forward and upward. Gravity and drag work to hold the plane back and bring it down to the ground. In order for an airplane to fly straight and level (or to fly at all), these forces must be balanced.

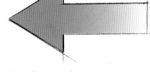

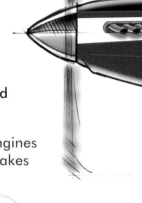

The force that creates speed is called **thrust**.

Airplane propellers and engines generate the thrust that makes the plane move forward.

A downhill skier will squeeze into a tight crouch to reduce drag and go faster.

©Karl Weatherly/CORBIS

PITCH, ROLL, AND YAW

An airplane—or any three-dimensional object—can turn in three main ways. Each of these can be thought of as rotation around a different axis.

Imagine each axis like earth's axis seen on a globe. The earth spins, or rotates, around this axis. In the same way, an airplane can spin around the three axes of rotation.

Is There a Doctor on the Plane?

Pitching, rolling, and yawing can all lead to airsickness, but the swiveling yaw motion might be the biggest factor. (And even pilots suffer from airsickness from time to time.)

Lift is the force that opposes gravity. An airplane must generate enough lift to overcome the force of gravity.

Although people have been flying airplanes for over 100 years, how lift works is still not completely understood.

Drag slows things down. Drag is the resistance to motion of two things rubbing together, such as a plane's surfaces and the air. Also, hitting oncoming air slows anything down. That's drag too. Airplane designers try to reduce drag by streamlining all the parts of a plane so that it can slip through the air easily.

If the amount of drag becomes larger than the amount of thrust, the plane will slow down. If the thrust is increased so that it is greater than the drag, the plane will speed up.

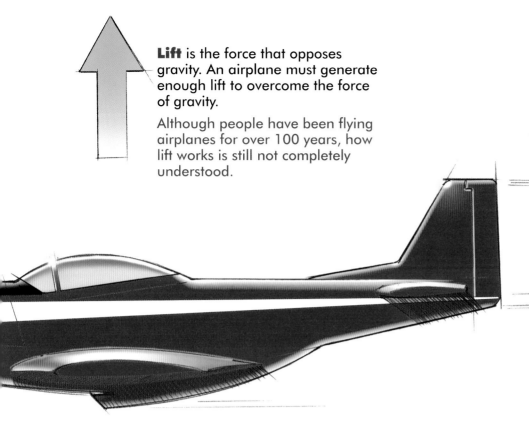

What goes up must come down. Everything in the universe exerts an attractive force on everything else. In other words, everything pulls everything else toward it. This force is called **gravity**.

The more mass an object has, the more it is affected by gravity. Gravity keeps us from floating away.

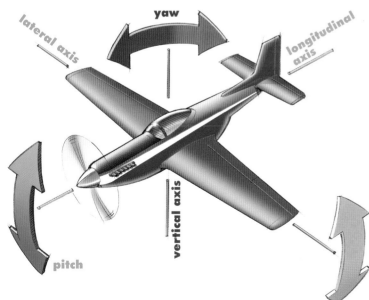

The **lateral axis** runs through the wings from tip to tip. When an airplane rotates around the lateral axis, it moves in a front-to-back tilt. This is called **pitch**.

The **longitudinal axis** runs through the airplane from nose to tail. When an airplane rotates around the longitudinal axis, it moves in a side-to-side tilt. This is called **roll**.

The **vertical axis** runs through the plane from top to bottom. When an airplane rotates around the vertical axis, it swivels side to side. This is called **yaw**.

Balancing Act

Pilots control the direction and rotation of the plane on all of the axes using the controls in the cockpit. Sound complicated? It is. Pilots have to handle different controls at the same time, to keep the forces in balance and make the plane move where and how they want. The next time you see an acrobatic aerial display, you'll be able to appreciate the skill of the pilots.

How Do Airplanes Fly?

Airplanes rely on principles of physics for flight. It also helps that their wings have a special shape that puts those principles to use.

All About Airfoils

The cross-section of a typical wing is called an airfoil. It's flat on the bottom and curved on top. As the wing moves through the air, the front, or leading, edge splits the air stream, forcing the air over the top and bottom of the wing. The air moving above the wing moves faster—but explaining how this works requires complex math.

According to a natural law called the Bernoulli effect, the pressure of a fluid (a liquid or a gas) decreases when the speed of the fluid increases. The air moving over the top of the

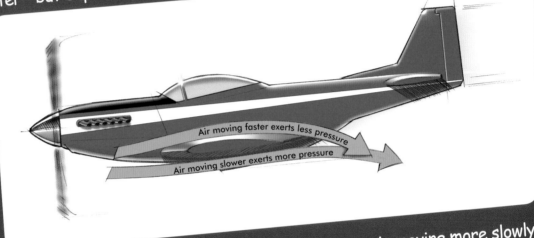

Air moving faster exerts less pressure

Air moving slower exerts more pressure

wing moves faster, so it has lower pressure. The air under the wing is moving more slowly and has a higher pressure. The wing (and plane) is pushed up by the higher pressure. And up means lift.

8

It's the Law

Sir Isaac Newton's third law of motion states that for every action, there is an equal and opposite reaction.

Hands-On Experiment

Try holding your hand out of a moving car and see what happens when you tilt it up from the horizontal. Like a tilted wing, the underside of your hand is struck by the oncoming air. When your hand deflects air downward, it's deflected upward.

More than just the Bernoulli effect is at work, however. A phenomenon called the Coanda effect has also been used to help explain lift. According to this principle, a fluid tends to follow the shape of the surface it is moving across.

In the early 20th century, the Romanian aerodynamicist Henri Coanda observed that a stream of air (or other fluid) emerging from a nozzle tends to follow a nearby curved or flat surface. See for yourself by holding the back of a spoon under a running faucet.

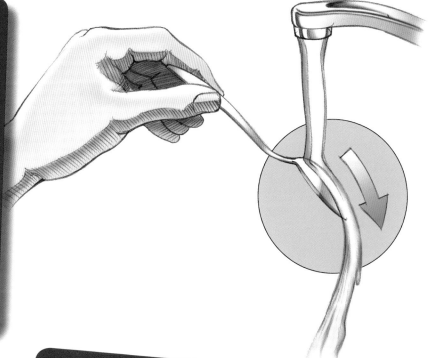

Because of the airfoil shape of the wing, and the Coanda effect, the air coming off the back, or trailing, edge is deflected downward. This brings us back to Newton and his law of actions and reactions. If the air moves downward off the back of the wing (action), the wing moves upward (reaction).

It's probably a combination of all these and other, still-mysterious principles that enables a plane to fly. As a matter of fact, we figured out how to fly before we figured out why we can!

Jet Demo
Blow up a balloon and hold it closed. What happens? Nothing, because the air pressure inside the balloon is equal in all directions. When you let it go, the balloon rushes forward as the air inside is pushed out backward. In a similar way, jet engines create thrust when exhaust shoots out the back.

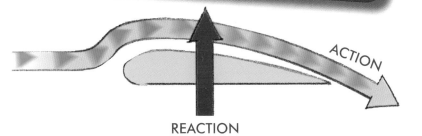

ACTION

REACTION

Full Tilt
There's another way Newton's third law comes into play to produce lift: As the wing moves through the air, it's tilted at a slight angle. As the air is deflected downward from the underside of the wing (the action), the wing moves upward (the reaction).

In the Pilot's Seat

Pilots' heads are anywhere but in the clouds. The complex instruments and monitors at their fingertips allow them to keep tight control. Early cockpits included just a few essential instruments. As the airplane evolved in complexity, so did the cockpit. Modern planes can have hundreds of gauges, lights, and switches. Keeping track of what's going on requires specialized training and steady nerves.

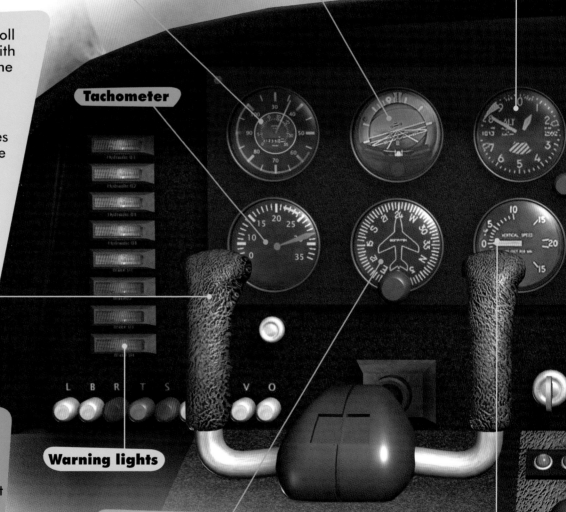

The **airspeed indicator** shows how fast the airplane is flying. Airspeed can differ from ground speed depending on the wind speed and the direction the airplane is flying in relation to the wind.

The **artificial horizon** or **electronic attitude direction indicator (EADI)** shows whether the airplane is pitching (tilting from front to back) or rolling (banking to the left or right).

The **altimeter** shows how high above sea level the airplane is flying.

The pilot controls the roll and pitch of a plane with subtle movements of the **control column** or **flight stick**.

Pushing or pulling the control column changes the pitch by moving the elevators up or down. This causes the plane's nose to point up or down. Turning the control column like a car's steering wheel affects the roll and steering by moving the ailerons. This causes the plane to dip one wingtip and raise the other.

Tachometer

Warning lights

Rudder pedals control the rudder. Pressing the left rudder pedal causes the rudder to swing to the left. Pressing the right rudder pedal causes the plane to turn right.

To help control turns, ascents, and descents, pilots depend on a compass-like instrument called a **directional gyroscope**.

The **vertical speed indicator** shows the speed of the plane's ascent or descent.

Cockpit Controls and What They Do

Cockpit Control	Control Surface	Motion
control stick (right and left)	ailerons	roll
control stick (front and back)	elevators	pitch
rudder pedals	rudder	yaw

The **fuel quantity gauge** and **oil temperature gauge** are among the most important gauges for monitoring engine performance.

The amount of fuel still in an airplane's tanks is always measured in pounds, not gallons or liters. To affect the balance of the plane, the pilot can shift fuel from one tank to another.

The **navigational display** is a compass, radar screen, and map all rolled into one. It shows where the plane is, where it's heading, and what weather patterns are ahead.

The needle of the **automatic direction finder (ADF)** points toward the destination's ground station. This radio-navigation instrument is also called a radio compass.

Outside air temperature

Magnetic compass

Flap indicator

When the plane detects that radar has bounced off of it, the **transponder** sends back a four-digit code along with altitude information. This lets air traffic controllers identify the aircraft, as it's displayed on their radar screens.

Navigation and anticollision lights

Voltmeter

Carburetor temperature gauge

Power levers are used to bring the engines up to speed. Each engine has a corresponding power lever.

Jumbo Jets

Jet planes have been popular since the 1950s. Huge jets, like the 747–400 shown here, are a part of daily life now. They're big enough to seat hundreds of passengers at a time and can lift incredible weights.

FLYING A GIANT

The 747-400 rumbles onto the runway and waits for clearance to take off. It's the pilot's first time at the controls and, looking at the instrument panels studded with gauges, switches, and dials, he hesitates. A deep breath, and he brings the four throttle controls to full power, releases the brakes on the 18 massive wheels—each one as tall as a man—and feels the 400-ton plane lurch forward.

The jumbo jet thunders down the runway. When the plane's speed reaches 180 mph, the nose of the plane starts to lift, so the pilot eases back on the flight stick to bring the tail elevators up. This gigantic bird is flying!

As soon as it's safe, the pilot retracts the landing gear and the flaps to reduce drag. The pilot levels off at about 35,000 feet, and as he does, the angle of attack is decreased. This reduces drag still further and lets the plane reach its cruising speed of nearly 600 mph.

A 747 has two sets of **ailerons**—a high-speed set near the fuselage and a low-speed set farther out. At low speeds both sets are used, but at high speeds the slight deflection caused by the inner ailerons is enough to help bank the plane (lean it into turns).

Each **engine** can produce more than 63,000 pounds of thrust. This means that each of the four engines works hard enough to suspend a massive concrete block that weighs over 30 tons!

Fuel tanks in the wings can hold more than 57,000 gallons. (That's more than 380,000 pounds!)

Into Thin Air

At 35,000 feet the air contains very little oxygen. That's why airliners pressurize their cabins before takeoff. The temperature up there is less than -50°F. Flipping a switch grimly called the "dead dog switch," the pilot can turn on heat in the cargo hold—just in case someone's family dog (or cat) is down there.

World's Largest Airliner

- Each engine is bigger than an SUV.
- The pilot's seat is as far off the ground as the third story of a house.
- Including fasteners, there are six million parts in a 747.
- At 150 feet long, the 747's economy section covers more distance than the Wright brothers' first flight.

©Roger Ressmeyer/CORBIS

Primarily passenger planes, 747s have also been used to transport space shuttles for NASA.

Once the 747-400 is cruising, the pilot switches on the **autopilot**, which can fly the plane without human input.

A modern-day 747 has a whopping 365 **lights, gauges, and switches**, down from 971 in earlier models.

13

©Reuters NewMedia Inc./CORBIS

Air Force One—the official airplane for the president of the United States—is a 747.

Private Jets

Jets aren't just for big crowds of people. If you have the money, you can buy your own private jet. These planes are fast and agile. Plus, you don't have to wait in line to buy a ticket. Of course, you might need your own pilot on standby.

The Show Must Go On

The singer has a concert in New York in only four and a half hours. No big deal. Except, at the moment, the singer's in Los Angeles. Awaiting her on the tarmac at the airport is her personal Cessna jet, a Citation X. It's fueled, flight-checked, and ready to go.

She steps into the plane and walks past the luxurious seats. The cabin feels more like a living room than an airplane. But she keeps walking all the way into the cockpit. This is her plane, and she's the only one who flies it. (Who says rock stars can't be pilots too? This one sure can.) Besides, the cabin might be fancy, but it's also a little cramped.

Once clearance is given for takeoff, the jet gets airborne quickly. Thirty minutes later it has reached 43,000 feet, its cruising altitude. At this altitude the Cessna is above most commercial air traffic and troublesome weather. The cruising speed is almost 600 mph. In a little over four hours the plane will descend into New York.

The **cockpit** of a Cessna Citation X shares many characteristics with cockpits of larger commercial jets.

14

Built for Speed

A Citation X can hit Mach .91 at 37,000 feet. That's almost as fast as the speed of sound. The Citation X needs a shorter runway than you might think—only about one-third the length needed for a 747.

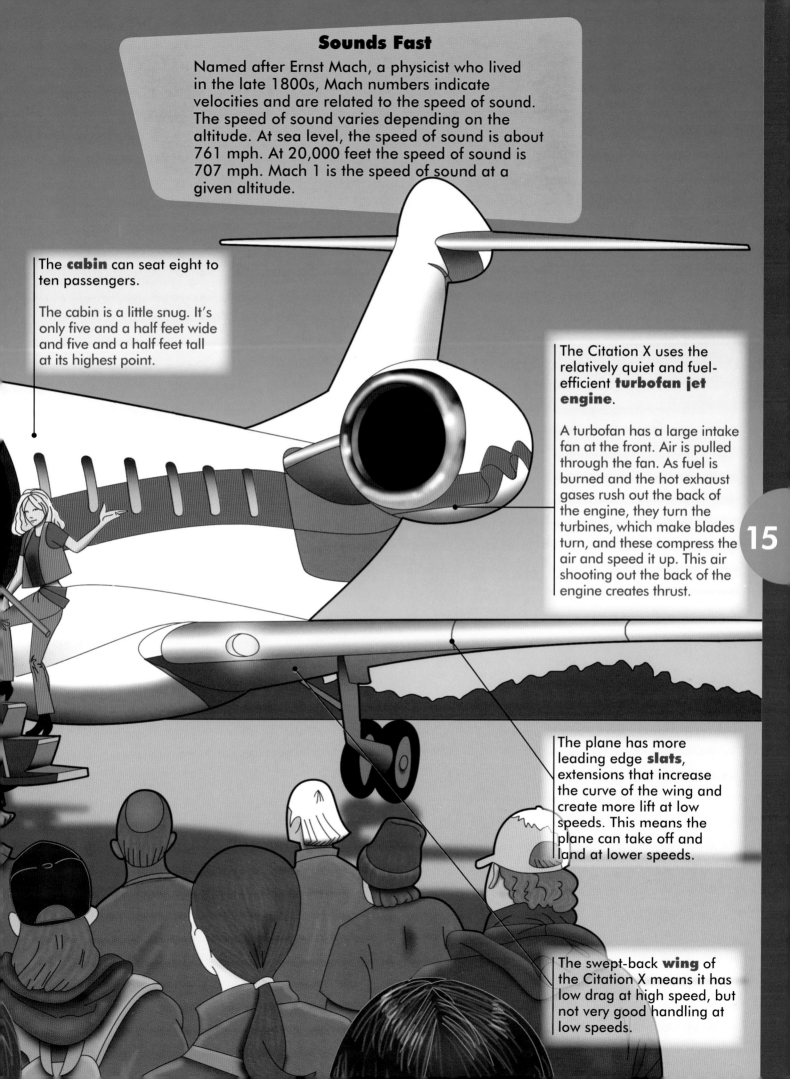

Sounds Fast

Named after Ernst Mach, a physicist who lived in the late 1800s, Mach numbers indicate velocities and are related to the speed of sound. The speed of sound varies depending on the altitude. At sea level, the speed of sound is about 761 mph. At 20,000 feet the speed of sound is 707 mph. Mach 1 is the speed of sound at a given altitude.

The **cabin** can seat eight to ten passengers.

The cabin is a little snug. It's only five and a half feet wide and five and a half feet tall at its highest point.

The Citation X uses the relatively quiet and fuel-efficient **turbofan jet engine**.

A turbofan has a large intake fan at the front. Air is pulled through the fan. As fuel is burned and the hot exhaust gases rush out the back of the engine, they turn the turbines, which make blades turn, and these compress the air and speed it up. This air shooting out the back of the engine creates thrust.

The plane has more leading edge **slats**, extensions that increase the curve of the wing and create more lift at low speeds. This means the plane can take off and land at lower speeds.

The swept-back **wing** of the Citation X means it has low drag at high speed, but not very good handling at low speeds.

Fighter Jets

Fighter jets (such as the Super Hornet, shown here) that are based on aircraft carriers are complex, versatile machines. They conduct air-to-air and air-to-ground combat missions, escort big bombers, and perform reconnaissance. All that, and they can take off from and land on a carrier's short and precarious runway.

Mission at Sea

The aircraft carrier sails across rough seas on a training exercise. A fighter jet is moved into position for takeoff. Its front wheel tow bar is attached to the steam-driven catapult.

In a burst of steam and fire, the jet is slammed forward, accelerating to over 180 mph in two seconds, and takes to the sky.

The pilot puts the plane into a steep climb, topping out at 45,000 feet. The Integrated Defensive Electronic Countermeasures system detects a simulated missile attack, and the pilot deploys decoy chaff. Tiny shreds of foil shoot out of the plane and disperse into a giant cloud of metallic confetti. The missile chases the chaff.

The jet's weapons system locks on to the missile and the pilot fires a Sidewinder air-to-air missile.

Moments later, the onboard computers confirm a "kill." Time to head back. Of course, landing on the carrier's deck is a tricky mission all in itself.

The **cockpit** of the Super Hornet is equipped with a touch-sensitive control display, a large multipurpose color LCD display showing tactical information, and two monochrome displays. A "hud" (head-up display) allows pilots to see what's happening without looking down at the monitors.

16

A **forward-looking infrared system** or **FLIR** ("fleer") allows the pilot to see ahead of the aircraft at night as if it were daytime.

arresting hook

An arresting hook hangs underneath the rear of a Super Hornet. When pilots make landings on a carrier, the hook catches on cables strung across the deck. Pilots come in at the slowest speeds they can manage, but as soon as they hit the deck, they go full throttle so that if they miss the cables they have enough power to take off again. The alternative is rolling off the deck and into the ocean.

Flying Ace

The Super Hornet carries the most advanced navigation, weapons guidance, and countermeasure systems available.

The Super Hornet is a flying **arsenal**. It carries one internal 20mm Vulcan cannon in the nose, and depending on the mission, can carry AIM-9 Sidewinder, AIM-7 Sparrow, and AIM-120 AMRAAM (Advanced Medium-Range Air-to-Air) missiles, and up to 17,750 pounds of ordnance, including "smart" bombs with laser, infrared, or GPS guidance!

Decoy chaff consists of tiny pieces of foil. When released from the plane, chaff forms a cloud even bigger than the plane. The missile's radar locks on to this new "target."

The carrier's **flight deck** isn't long enough for Super Hornets to take off in the usual way, so they get a little assistance in the form of a catapult.

Under the deck of the carrier are two pistons attached to a shuttle that runs in a slot in the deck. The shuttle attaches to the nose gear of the plane. When enough pressure has built up around the pistons, a crew member called the "shooter" releases the shuttle, slamming the plane forward.

Bush Planes

Bush planes are propeller-driven workhorses. They're small, but powerful and reliable. Adventurers, explorers, and people living in remote areas depend on bush planes to get them where they need to go, and to deliver essential supplies.

The Wild Blue Yonder

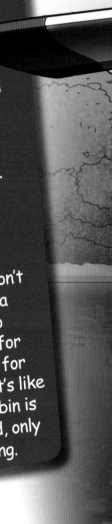

The remote valley fills with the drone of an engine as the Beaver clears the ridge and lands on the small lake. The Garrison family lives 75 miles from the nearest town. The weekly mail and supply deliveries provided by the bush plane are their main contact with the outside world.

As the Beaver draws up alongside the dock, the family runs down to greet the pilot. Winter is on the way and the Garrisons can't wait to unload their special cargo: a new generator and a couple of 55-gallon drums of diesel fuel.

The pilot is ready to leave, but she won't be going alone: The Garrisons' husky needs a minor operation and the pilot has agreed to bring him to the vet. The Beaver pulls out for takeoff and, after skimming over the lake for 1,000 feet, rises gracefully into the air. It's like a swan, and not much faster. The small cabin is noisy, but the eagle's-eye view of the land, only a few thousand feet below, is breathtaking.

Snow Business
Bush planes can be outfitted with skis. They let pilots land on ice and compact snow. In some models, the tires fit through holes in the skis, so the planes can land on runways or snow.

©Paul A. Souders/CORBIS

One Tough Plane

The Beaver was built solid as a rock. It soon earned the nickname "the flying pickup truck."

The expansive **surface area** of the wings means a Beaver can generate lots of lift. The large wings also give the plane short takeoff and landing (STOL) ability, even with heavy loads. All that makes it the perfect bush plane, capable of hauling lots of cargo or people into and out of the wilderness.

One factor of the Beaver's success is its **high lift wing configuration**. The wings are mounted high, above the cockpit, so the pilot can see below. And that's perfect for making landings on uneven terrain or small lakes.

Floats give the plane the ability to make water takeoffs and landings. Some bush planes are "convertibles," too: With the flick of a switch, the pilot lowers retractable wheels from within the floats. Now the plane can safely land on solid ground.

Sometimes pilots strap cargo (even canoes!) to the floats. Because bush planes don't fly very fast, cargo carried this way will survive the trip.

The Beaver uses an **internal combustion piston engine**, similar to the ones used in cars.

As a piston moves down, it sucks a mixture of air and fuel into the space above it. When the piston rises, the air-fuel mixture is compressed and then ignited by a spark plug. The resulting explosion pushes the piston down with tremendous force. The pistons are connected to a crankshaft, which is connected to the propeller. The result of all those mini explosions is a spinning propeller that pulls the plane forward.

VSTOL Planes

When there's no conventional runway—at sea or on the front lines of combat—special airplanes are vital. At times like that, you need a plane with the ability to become airborne in limited space. This need led to the evolution of the fighter known as the Harrier.

TURNING THE TABLES

The forest calm is shattered by the roar of a mighty Rolls-Royce Pegasus turbofan engine. A strange shape rises above the tree canopy, as if lifted by wires. The plane turns 90 degrees south and smoothly transitions into forward flight. In a matter of seconds the Harrier disappears from sight as the pilot puts it into full throttle. His mission in this exercise is to provide aerial support for the ground troops.

As a part of the "game," the jet is attacked by another plane, enabling the Harrier pilot to show off his skill and his plane's true colors. The pilot performs a trick called VIFF—"vectoring in forward flight." At high speed, the pilot reverses the exhaust gas nozzles so they point forward. The jet rapidly decelerates, as if the pilot had slammed the brakes.

The attacking plane overshoots the Harrier and is now a wide-open target.
Hunter becomes prey.
Score another one for the agile Harrier.

When the Harrier is hovering, it relies solely on **nozzles** to stay in the air. The wings are useless during hovering, and this makes the jet highly unstable. To overcome this problem, nozzles that shoot out exhaust gases are placed in the front of the plane, at the back, and at the wingtips. The pilot operates these to control the plane's pitch, roll, and yaw.

VSTOL

The most remarkable feature of the Harrier is its ability to take off and land without any runway at all. (Of course, that is exactly what a helicopter does, but a helicopter can't fly at close to the speed of sound.) This ability is called VSTOL, which stands for "vertical or short takeoff and landing."

Take a Flying Leap

Small British Navy aircraft carriers are equipped with a ramp at the end of their flight decks. This enables Harriers to roll forward and "leap" off the deck carrying more fuel and weapons than they could if they took off vertically from a flat deck.

The Harrier uses an off-the-shelf Pegasus **turbofan engine**, with one major modification: four nozzles, two on each side of the plane.

The nozzles rotate (vector) to change the thrust of the engine: down for VSTOL, to the rear for conventional flight, and to the front to decelerate quickly. By carefully adjusting the throttle and the nozzle angle, a pilot can fly a Harrier from 50 mph backward to over 600 mph forward.

Some variations of the Harrier can carry the same weight in **bombs** as the B-17 Flying Fortress.

World War II Fighters

Mustangs flew as escorts for Flying Fortresses, the huge B-17 heavy bombers. Due to their amazing range, P-51D Mustangs were able to protect bombers on raids into the heart of Nazi Germany during World War II.

A Bomber's Little Friend

The mission: Bomb a munitions factory in southern Germany. Even though B-17s are heavily armed, the Mustangs provide their real defense. The B-17, with a maximum speed of about 290 mph, is vulnerable to Messerschmitts and other enemy fighters.

Soaring closer and closer to the factory, through cloudless skies, the crew of the B-17 feels comparatively safe, escorted by the Red Tail Angels. High over the bombers, like sharks swimming above a whale, the 332nd Fighter Group keeps a close lookout for enemy fighters. The men in their Mustangs know that their planes are more than a match for anything the enemy can throw up against them. And their six machine guns and tank-piercing ammunition can help them make their case.

Dark specks on the horizon zoom closer and take shape—Messerschmitts, and they're looking for a fight!

A Mustang pilot yells into his radio, "Push the throttle to the wall!" and the Mustangs accelerate to meet the enemy.

The Tuskegee Airmen's nickname, "Red Tail Angels," comes from the fact that the **tails** of their Mustangs were painted bright red. Bomber crews also called fighter escorts their "Little Friends."

One end of the **radio antenna** was attached to the tail. From there, it passed through the canopy. The other end was attached to the back of the pilot's seat.

Cool Under Fire

When dropping from high altitude in a steep dive, a pilot had to have lightning-fast reactions to avoid being torn to shreds by enemy fire before he even knew what was happening.

22

The Fighting 332nd

The Tuskegee Airmen of the 332nd Fighter Group were the first all-African-American squadron to serve in World War II. In 200 missions where the Tuskegee Airmen were bomber escorts, not a single bomber was lost to enemy aircraft.

©CORBIS

The Twin Mustang was developed to handle longer missions. With its two side-by-side fuselages, it carried two pilots. The pilots could take shifts, so the plane could stay in action longer.

The **bubble canopy** of the Mustang gave good all-around visibility, crucial for a World War II fighter pilot.

Some Mustangs were equipped with a special **bar** for releasing the canopy completely in an emergency.

23

P-51D Mustangs had three **machine guns** mounted in each wing. In earlier Mustang models, the guns were tilted to the side, but this caused them to jam. So in the P-51D, the guns were mounted flat.

A **camera** in the left wing filmed the action whenever the pilot fired the guns. The footage was used to confirm hits on enemy planes and help the pilots train.

History of Flight

Penguins, ostriches, kiwis—humans share one important thing with these birds. *We* can't fly either. While flightless birds haven't lost a minute of sleep about their inability to fly, countless people have devoted their lives to the dream and passion of flight. Here are some milestones in the quest for flight.

BACK TO THE DRAWING BOARD

In the late 1400s, Italian visionary Leonardo da Vinci devised flying machines that were far ahead of their time. Some of his designs were meant to be powered, some were meant to work like gliders or parachutes. His "aerial screw" is thought to be the predecessor to the helicopter. He also invented an aircraft that beat its wings, like a bird.

Unfortunately, if he had gone ahead and built these machines, they probably wouldn't have worked. Humans just aren't strong enough to provide the force needed to achieve lift with these machines. Maybe he knew this: He also worked on a powerful spring to power some of his inventions.

ENGINE-FREE ZONE

Sir George Cayley built and flew the first model glider that had wings and a tail, in 1804. His glider was the forerunner for future aircraft design.

Just like that glider, today's gliders have no engines, so their pilots search the sky for rising columns of air called thermals, which they circle to gain altitude, just like a buzzard does. Pilots look for hills—one place you might expect to find thermal updrafts—or birds that have hitched a ride on a thermal. A good pilot can glide for hours and cover many miles.

TWELVE HISTORIC SECONDS

The world's first successful, powered plane was the Flyer, designed by Orville and Wilbur Wright. The plane was made of wood, baling wire, and muslin cloth. But this humble plane was good enough to take off under its own power, glide in controlled flight, and land in one piece. The first flight lasted 12 seconds and spanned just over 120 feet. Later, on that same morning of December 17, 1903, the Flyer was overturned and crushed by a gust of wind.

LUCKY LINDY

In 1927, Charles Lindbergh became the first person to fly solo across the North Atlantic. It took him over 33 hours, without sleep, to pilot the Spirit of St. Louis into the record books. There was also prize money at stake: Lucky Lindy won $25,000 for his feat.

BREAKING THE BARRIER

High over the California desert, Chuck Yeager piloted the Bell X-1 on its history-making flight across the sound barrier. It was 1947, and the X-1 became the first plane to fly faster than the speed of sound. The Air Force kept the news secret until the following year.

Into the Record Books

Some planes are built to help designers understand new types of engines or wings. Some are built purely for the fun of flying them. Here are five experimental planes of the recent past— and the near future—that made their mark.

WOODEN GIANT

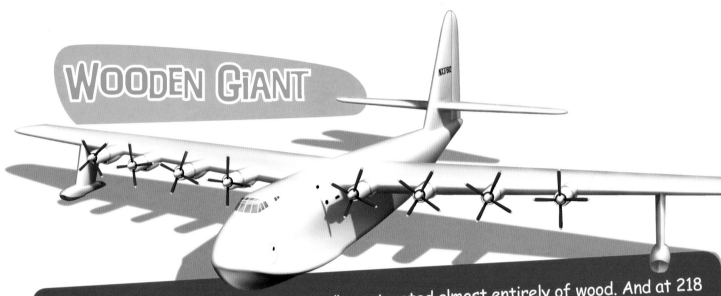

The Spruce Goose was a "flying boat" constructed almost entirely of wood. And at 218 feet long, with a wingspan of 320 feet, it's still one of the largest planes ever flown. It could take off and land on water. When it flew low over the water, a cushion of air formed under the wings. This helped keep the plane airborne. The Goose was flown for the first and only time in 1947.

NONSTOP VOYAGE

In 1986 the Rutan Voyager made the first flight around the world without refueling. The Voyager made its around-the-world trip in nine days, three minutes, and forty-four seconds. (This is still the longest nonstop, unrefueled flight in history.) To accomplish this, the Voyager needed to be as light as possible. In fact, there's no metal at all in its frame. To make it around the world, the plane also needed huge amounts of fuel. Most of the plane's takeoff weight was in its seventeen fuel tanks.

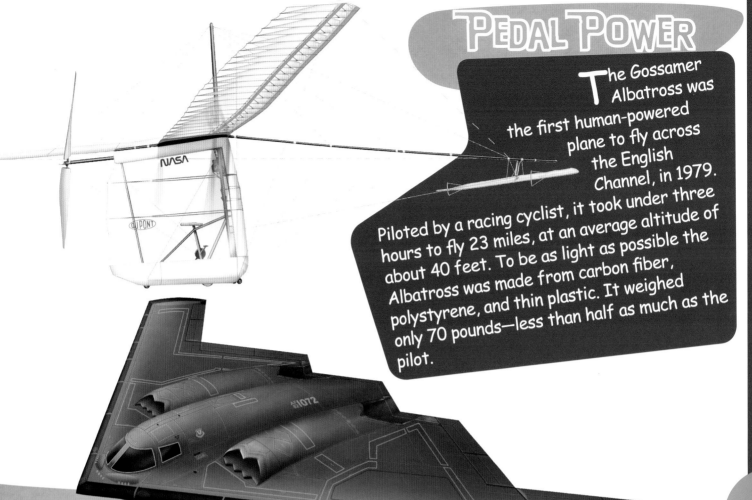

PEDAL POWER

The Gossamer Albatross was the first human-powered plane to fly across the English Channel, in 1979. Piloted by a racing cyclist, it took under three hours to fly 23 miles, at an average altitude of about 40 feet. To be as light as possible the Albatross was made from carbon fiber, polystyrene, and thin plastic. It weighed only 70 pounds—less than half as much as the pilot.

GHOST IN THE SKY

The bat-shaped B-2 Spirit stealth bomber is one of the sneakiest planes ever. It flies at "only" about 600 mph, but "stealth" technology makes it almost invisible to enemy radar. It's covered with a material that absorbs radar signals instead of bouncing them back. It cools its exhaust and vents it out the top, so it won't be detectable by infrared "eyes" on the ground. These are just some of its tricks.

HIGH-SPEED EXPERIMENT

NASA has a plane in the works that will be almost as important to the history of flight as the Wright brothers' Flyer: The X-43 might fly at Mach 10—ten times the speed of sound—at an altitude of 100,000 feet. It will use an experimental type of engine called a scramjet, which scoops oxygen out of the atmosphere and mixes it with hydrogen. If commercial models of the X-43 are ever built, you'll be able to cross the Atlantic Ocean in minutes instead of hours.

Assembly Instructions

The parts included in your Flight Test Lab:

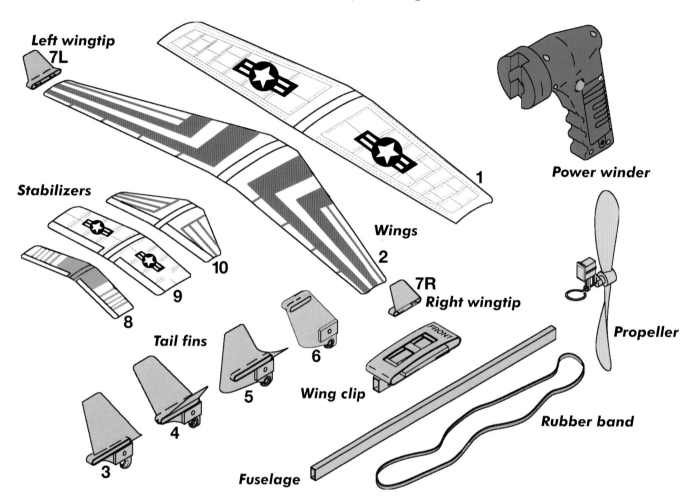

Left wingtip
7L

Power winder

1

Wings

2

Stabilizers

10

9

8

7R
Right wingtip

Propeller

Tail fins

6

5

Wing clip

Rubber band

4

3

Fuselage

Battery Cautions

- To ensure proper safety and operation, the battery replacement must always be done by an adult.
- Never let a child use this product unless the battery door is secure.
- Keep all batteries away from small children, and immediately dispose of any batteries safely.
- Batteries are small objects and could be ingested.
- Nonrechargeable batteries are not to be recharged.
- Rechargeable batteries are to be removed from toy before being charged.
- Rechargeable batteries are only to be charged under adult supervision.
- Different types of batteries or new and used batteries are not to be mixed.
- Only batteries of the same or equivalent types as recommended are to be used.
- Do not mix alkaline, standard (carbon-zinc), or rechargeable (nickel-cadmium) batteries.
- Batteries are to be inserted with the correct polarity.
- Exhausted batteries are to be removed from the toy.
- The supply terminals are not to be short-circuited.

INSTALLING THE BATTERIES

Unscrew the battery compartment door. Insert two new AAA alkaline or carbon-zinc batteries. Make sure both batteries are inserted the right way, according to the diagram inside the battery compartment. Slide the battery compartment door back on and screw it in place. Don't use excessive force or the wrong type or size of screwdriver.

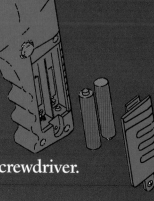

These steps show you how to build and fine-tune the Mustang, but the steps for any plane are very similar.

Step 1

Slide the wing clip about halfway up the fuselage. The front of the wing clip is marked FRONT, and the wing slot is on top.

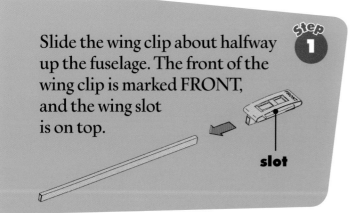

slot

Step 2

Attach the propeller and tail fin (part 5) to the fuselage. The propeller goes on the front of the fuselage, the tail fin on the rear. Hold the tail fin by the bottom only, or else it could break when you push it onto the fuselage.

hook

hook

Make sure the hooks under the propeller and the tail fin are on the bottom of the fuselage.

Step 3

Insert the wings (part 1) into the wing slot. Carefully work the wing through until it's centered. Insert the stabilizer (part 9) into the slot in the tail fin. Carefully work it through until it's centered.

The side of the wings and stabilizer that's more pointed is the front.

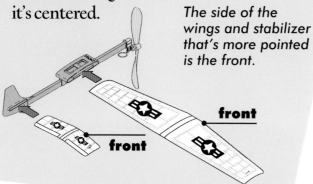

front

front

Step 4

Slip the rubber band onto the hook under the propeller and the hook under the tail fin.

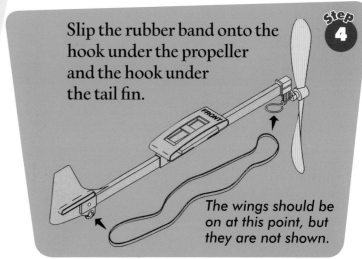

The wings should be on at this point, but they are not shown.

Step 5

Check the alignment. Looking at the plane from the rear, make sure the wings and stabilizers are centered. Make sure the tail fin is straight up and down.

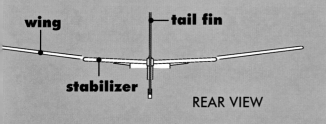

wing
tail fin
stabilizer

REAR VIEW

Step 6

Balance the plane. Each wing has two balance points printed on the underside.

Bottom of wing

Hold the plane up with a fingertip directly under each balance point. If the plane is balanced, it will sit level when you hold it this way.

29

Step 7

If the nose drops when you support the plane on the balance points (see step 6), move the wing clip forward a little.

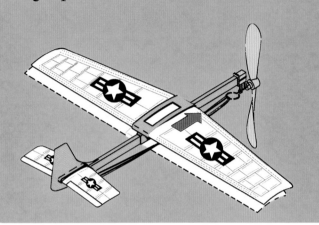

Step 8

If the tail drops when you support the plane on the balance points (see step 6), move the wing clip back a little.

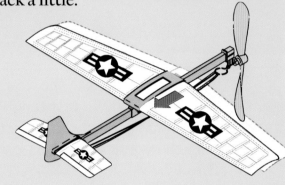

Step 9

Insert the propeller of the assembled plane into the notch in the winder. Press the winder button to wind the propeller. When the rubber band is as tight as it should be, the winder will automatically stop winding.

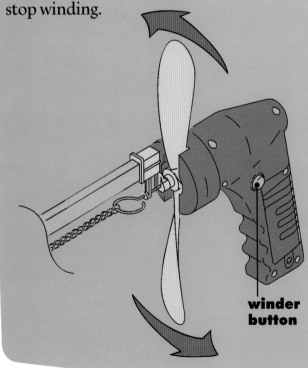

winder button

Step 10

Now you're ready for takeoff! (Outdoors only.) Don't throw the plane forcefully, like you'd throw a ball. Instead, push it forward through the air and let it go.

FINE-TUNING

Turn to the Troubleshooting section on the inside of the back cover for more fine-tuning tips and advice.

Experiment until your plane is flying perfectly.

With your Flight Test Lab you can assemble the four airplanes shown below.
The illustrations lay out the parts you'll need for assembling each plane. Once you've
built them all, you can mix tails, wings, and stabilizers to create your own designs.

MUSTANG

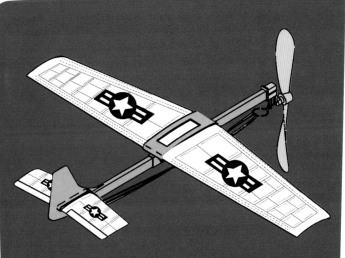

- **Fuselage**
- **Wing clip**
- **Propeller**
- **Tail fin** (5)
- **Wings** (1)
- **Stabilizer** (9)
- **Rubber band**

747

- **Fuselage**
- **Wing clip**
- **Propeller**
- **Tail fin** (3)
- **Wings** (2)
- **Wing tips** (7L and 7R)
- **Stabilizer** (10)
- **Rubber band**

SUPER HORNET

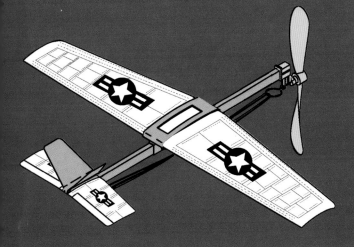

- **Fuselage**
- **Wing clip**
- **Propeller**
- **Tail fin** (4)
- **Wings** (1)
- **Stabilizer** (9)
- **Rubber band**

CITATION X

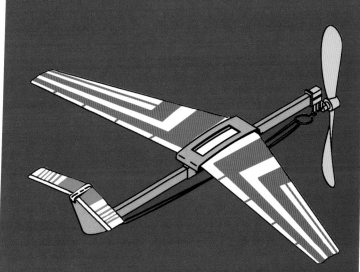

- **Fuselage**
- **Wing clip**
- **Propeller**
- **Tail fin** (6)
- **Wings** (2)
- **Stabilizer** (8)
- **Rubber band**

Glossary
of Important Airplane Terms

Afterburner
Part of a jet engine used to increase thrust for short periods during takeoff and combat emergencies. Fuel is sprayed into the jet exhaust for an instant power boost.

Ailerons
Movable panels on the back edge of a wing. When moved up or down, they cause the airplane to roll, or bank to the right or left.

Aircraft
Any vehicle, such as an airplane, hang glider, hot-air balloon, or helicopter, that travels through the air.

Airfoil
A surface with a curved top that creates an upward push, or lift, when moving through the air.

Altitude
Height above sea level.

Avionics
Electronics that are specially designed for use in aircraft.

Bank
To lean an aircraft to one side as it goes into a turn.

Cockpit
The small compartment in an aircraft where the pilot sits to control the flight.

Drag
The force that slows down an object's movement because of friction between the object and whatever it's moving across or through.

Elevator
A movable surface on the back edge of a horizontal stabilizer that makes an airplane climb or dive.

Empennage
The tail section of an airplane, including horizontal and vertical stabilizers and the rudder.

Exhaust
The parts of an engine through which waste gases escape. Also, the gases themselves. In a jet engine the exhaust produces thrust.

Fuselage
The main body or section of an airplane or helicopter.

Glider
A craft without engines, having long wings to ride the wind.

Lift
A force pushing upward, such as the upward push created when an airfoil or wing moves through the air.

Navigation
The practice of finding one's way from one point to another.

Pitch
Up-and-down rocking motion of an aircraft, controlled by the elevators.

Propeller
Blades projecting from a spinning center that pull air in from the front and push it backward.

Radar
RAdio Detecting And Ranging: a method of detecting aircraft using radio waves, which bounce back off the aircraft and form a picture of it on a screen.

Retractable undercarriage
Landing legs and wheels of an aircraft, designed to fold away into the fuselage or wings during flight.

Roll
Side-to-side tilting motion of an aircraft, controlled by ailerons.

Rudder
A movable surface on the tail of an aircraft, used for steering left or right.

Supersonic
Able to fly faster than the speed of sound.

Thermal
Rising mass of warm air used by gliders to gain height.

Thrust
The force that propels or drives something forward.

Yaw
Side-to-side swiveling motion of an aircraft, controlled by the rudder.

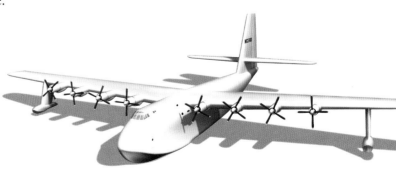